Ella Minnow
and the
New Fish
Written by
John D. Avera
Illustrated by
Crystal Johnson

Ella Minnow and the New Fish

Hydra Publications
1310 Meadowridge Trail
Goshen, KY 40026

www.hydrapublications.com

Acknowledgments

This book is dedicated to Dylan Wagers, Chad and Connor Ratliff and many others who struggle everyday with a disability. I would like to thank God for everything that he has done for me. I would also like to thank my family for their support and encouragement.

In memory of my nephew:

Spencer Avery Sapp.

August 28, 1998- November 28, 2007

Also by John D. Avera

Ella Minnow Peed

A great resource to combat bullying.

Given a five-star rating by Reader's Favorite.

Hey Ella, shouted her friend Billy Bass.

Did you see the new fish in the school? He only has one fin, He said as he chuckled.

What do you mean he only has one fin? Ella questioned.

Really, he only has one fin, AND when he swims, he swims in a circle! He said as he giggled.

Ella wondered what Billy was talking about as he swam away shouting to his other friends what he had seen. The only thing that Ella knew was that all the fish were talking about this new fish and what he looked like. Ella remembered how she was treated by the other fish and how scary it was on her first day of school.

I am going to find this new fish and ask him to be my friend, Ella thought to herself.

Ella swam through the school looking for the new fish. She was hearing all about the "fish with only one fin," because it seemed like everyone was talking about it.

She met in the hallway to talk to Emily and Belle, the two other minnows that had transferred to Lake Cumberland fish school. Ella had helped these two girls when they came from the fish farm in the neighboring county. They were scared to enter the new environment, but Ella showed them that the other students would accept them for what they were.

Even Emily and Belle were talking about him. No one had ever seen a fish with just one fin until now.

I saw him this morning, and there was a new teacher swimming beside him. I guess to keep him swimming straight. He was a slow swimmer and could barely stay straight with the help of the teacher, said Belle.

When I saw him, he was not being helped by the teacher and was just swimming in circles, cried Emily.

Well, I have yet to see the new fish, and personally, I can't wait to meet him, not because I care that he is different, but because I would like to be his friend and show him around, said Ella.

All three girls swam to the lunch room, where they met with Kameron the bluegill, to eat. After going through the line and getting lunch, they went to find their seat.

These new lunches here at school are terrible, said Emily.

They are supposed to be healthy, but mostly they are awful! replied Belle.

It is some kind of new law that the president has put into place, Kameron said, *I know that I really don't like them.*

All four girls agreed and laughed and giggled as they ate their food.

While the other girls were talking about the food, boys, and life as a young girl, Ella glanced out the cafeteria window into the hallway. For a moment she saw a couple of fish that she had never seen before. But it was only for a moment, so she decided to let it go and kept talking and having fun with her friends.

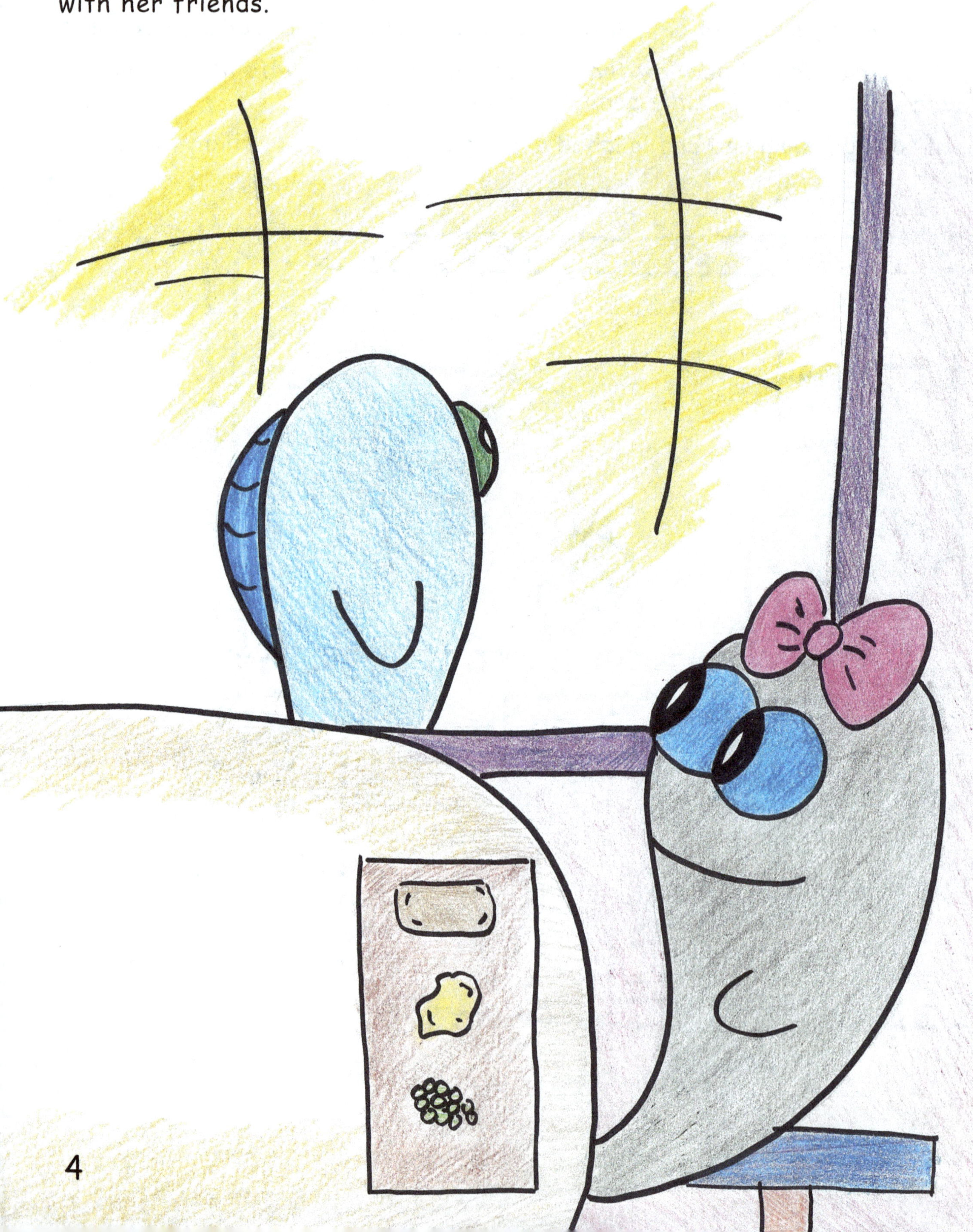

4

Later in the day after math class, Ella was headed out for recess. This was her favorite part of the day. She was going to try out for the speed swimming team. Ella loved recess because she could sing as loud as she wanted, play with her friends, but the last few weeks she had been practicing for the swim team tryouts. Ella swam over to the other side of the lake away from the other fish so she could swim some laps and not be bothered, when she saw that same fish she had seen at lunch.

Ella swam over to the new boy and said, "*Hi, my name is Ella, what is your name?*"

The new fish looked at her and said, *my name is Dylan*. Dylan was a carp that you could tell was not like the other ones in the school. One thing that Ella noticed, was that her friend Billy was right, the new fish does only have one fin. That was the weirdest thing that Ella had ever seen, she had never met someone with only one fin. Ella just stared at the missing fin forever, it seemed, while Dylan was talking.

When suddenly he said, *I was born that way.*

Who..Whaa…Whaa…what? Ella answered as she was startled out of her deep concentration.

Yeah, I was born with only one fin, Dylan said. *It's okay though, I can do almost everything that you can do, just in a different way.*

Ella didn't know what to think about what Dylan had said, but knew that she had to do something to help him.

Ella said to Dylan, *Do you have any friends here at Lake Cumberland?*

Dylan responded, *I have a few but they go to another school down- stream, most of my friends are still at the fish farm.*

Oh, Ella said, *would you like to be my friend? I can show you around and help you out.*

That would be nice, Dylan answered, I would like to be your friend.

Recess was over and Ella didn't get to practice, but she did meet a new friend so she was fine with missing out on swimming.

Ella thought all day about how awful and how hard it must be to only have one fin, and what she could do to help him. Many thoughts were going through her mind.

Later that day, while leaving the school to go home, Ella saw Dylan swimming while the older fish, she had seen earlier that day, watched. Sure enough she saw that he was swimming in a complete circle. He was really fast but was making a complete circle around the older fish.

"Oh, no. I really need to help him. He must have been making up the story of being able to do what I can do because he was embarrassed," Ella said with sincere concern.

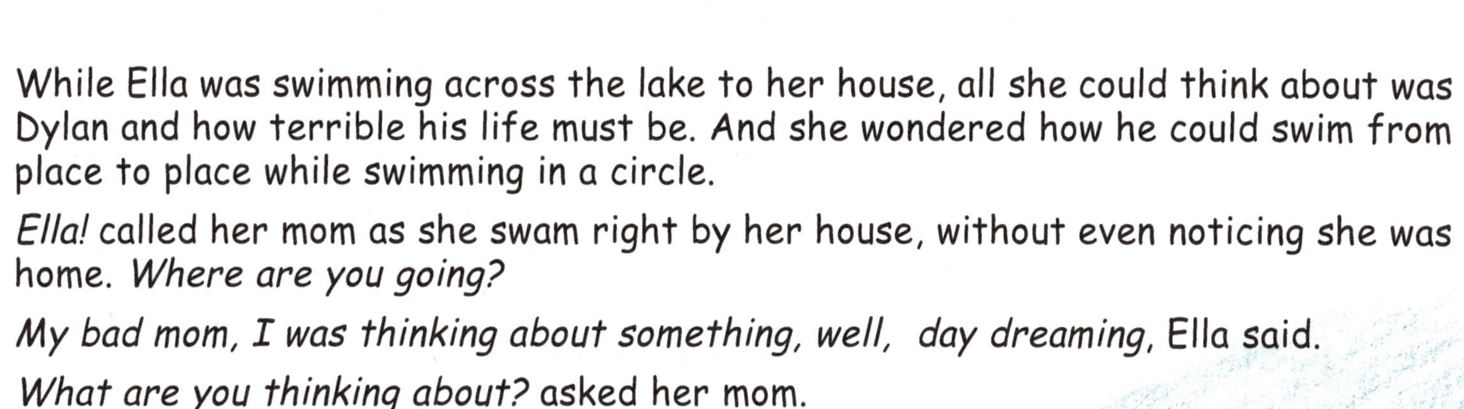

While Ella was swimming across the lake to her house, all she could think about was Dylan and how terrible his life must be. And she wondered how he could swim from place to place while swimming in a circle.

Ella! called her mom as she swam right by her house, without even noticing she was home. *Where are you going?*

My bad mom, I was thinking about something, well, day dreaming, Ella said.

What are you thinking about? asked her mom.

I was just thinking about this new boy at our school, answered Ella.

Looks like someone must have their first crush, her mom sang in a high pitched voice while smiling as big as a whale.

No mom, stop, I do not! Why would you say that? Ella responded to her mother.

I am just kidding Ella, parents like to have a little fun with their kids you know.

Come on in, dinner will be ready in a few minutes, why don't you go ahead and do your homework? You have swim team practice later. You know there is a big race coming up soon. Her mom reminded her.

After finishing her homework and eating dinner, Ella got her swim cap and everything that she needed for swim team practice and put it in her bag. She swam across the lake with her mom and dad and headed to practice.

Today was the day that anyone could come and tryout for the swim team. Ella was one of the best swimmers in the school and had won many competitions. Mostly because she was small and quick.

Looking throughout the pool she could see all types of fish swimming around and working out.

Wow! There are a lot of fish trying out this year. Ella exclaimed as she looked across the pool.

Ella soon noticed the new fish, Dylan. He was going into the coach's office with the coach and two other fish.

I wonder if that is his mom and dad? Ella whispered to herself.

You're next Ella! Said Emily.

Okay! Replied Ella.

Ella dove into the pool and went on with her tryout for the team. She did very well, as usual, and knew that she had probably made the team just by seeing the coach's reaction.

The next day, Ella went into the school and saw Dylan.

Ella you're not going to believe this! He said excitedly.

Believe what, Dylan? Ella said.

She could see the excitement in his face and could really tell by the way he talked.

I made the team! Dylan screamed while he swam around in the fastest small circle that you have ever seen.

What team? questioned Ella.

The swim team, I am on the speed team with you! He said after swimming in a circle so much that he was now dizzy and his eyes were still spinning around, even though he was still.

I am proud of you Dylan, Ella said, but she could not figure out what he was going to do.

Ella said, *"see ya' Dylan!"* and swam away to go on with her day.

While she was heading to her first class she thought to herself, "that must be why he and his parents went into the coaches office, to see if Dylan can be on the team."

She then said out loud, *He must be the new team manager, yeah that makes sense, Dylan is the team manager.*

After making the conclusion the Dylan was the team manager Ella was satisfied and went on with her day.

Later that evening all the fish that had made the team were practicing for the big swim meet later that week. But there was one fish that was not at any practice, Dylan. He was always coming into the pool area as everyone else was leaving.

As Ella swam by with Belle and Emily by her side she called out, *Hey, Dylan!*

Hey! Dylan replied as he swam in between his parents.

Dylan says he is on the swim team, but I haven't seen him at any of the practices until the end, said Ella to her friends.

What do you think he is doing here after we leave? Belle questioned.

I am thinking that he is the team manager and that he is there to help the coach get cleaned up and shut the pool down. Or, maybe he is talking to him about what he can do to help at the meet this weekend, Ella answered.

At school the next day, while Ella was sitting in choir class, an announcement came over the intercom.

Listen up! said Mr. C.

"Due to there being a swim meet tomorrow at school, Coach Stephens has decided that there will be no practice tonight so the team will be able to rest. Thank you and have a nice day."

Ella was relieved that there was no practice and that she could take the day off.

When Ella got home, she heard her dad say that he was going to the pool to set some things up for the big meet. As she swam to her room she reached for the phone and dialed Dylan's house.

"Hello?" said an adult voice on the phone.

Is Dylan there? asked Ella.

No he is at swim practice, answered the deep voice on the other end of the phone, Can I take a message?

Yes please, could you tell him that Ella called? She asked.

I sure will, he replied.

Ella was so confused, I thought there was no practice today? What would Dylan be doing there today? There is nothing to clean up.

Ella swam down the stairs of her house to the dining room where her family was getting ready to eat dinner.

While eating dinner, Ella was still confused about the whole practice situation and why Dylan was never there if he was on the team. Ella was just sitting there chewing and chewing and staring off into space when her mom said, Ella!

 Ella jumped a little and asked her dad, *Would you care if I swam with you to the pool?*

That would be fine, Ell, replied her dad. *Is that what you have been thinking about? Are you wanting to get in another workout after all?* He questioned.

Something like that, said Ella.

On the way over, Ella's dad was talking about all things that had happened to him that day when he asked, *So are you ready for the race this weekend?*

Ella made no reponse.

Ella. Ella? Ella! Said her dad.

Oh, sorry, what were you saying? Replied Ella.

What are you thinking about so much today, Ella? asked her dad.

Just thinking about the new fish at school. We didn't have practice today and he said that he did. I think he helps clean up after we finish, but why would he be there today? Ella questioned.

Not really sure, Ella, maybe we will see him there, said her dad.

When they reached the pool, the first thing Ella did was look for her friend Dylan. She noticed him going into the coach's office to meet with Coach Stephens.

What is that coat he is wearing? She asked her dad.

It looks like some kind of special swimming vest or something, her dad replied.

Swimming vest? I wonder what it's for? Ella asked.

Ella's dad answered, *It's probably how he swims at these meets. I am sure you have seen him wearing it at school.*

But Ella had not. She had only seen him swimming in a circle or swimming with an adult fish by his side.

Ella and her dad went home to get some sleep for the big race the next day.

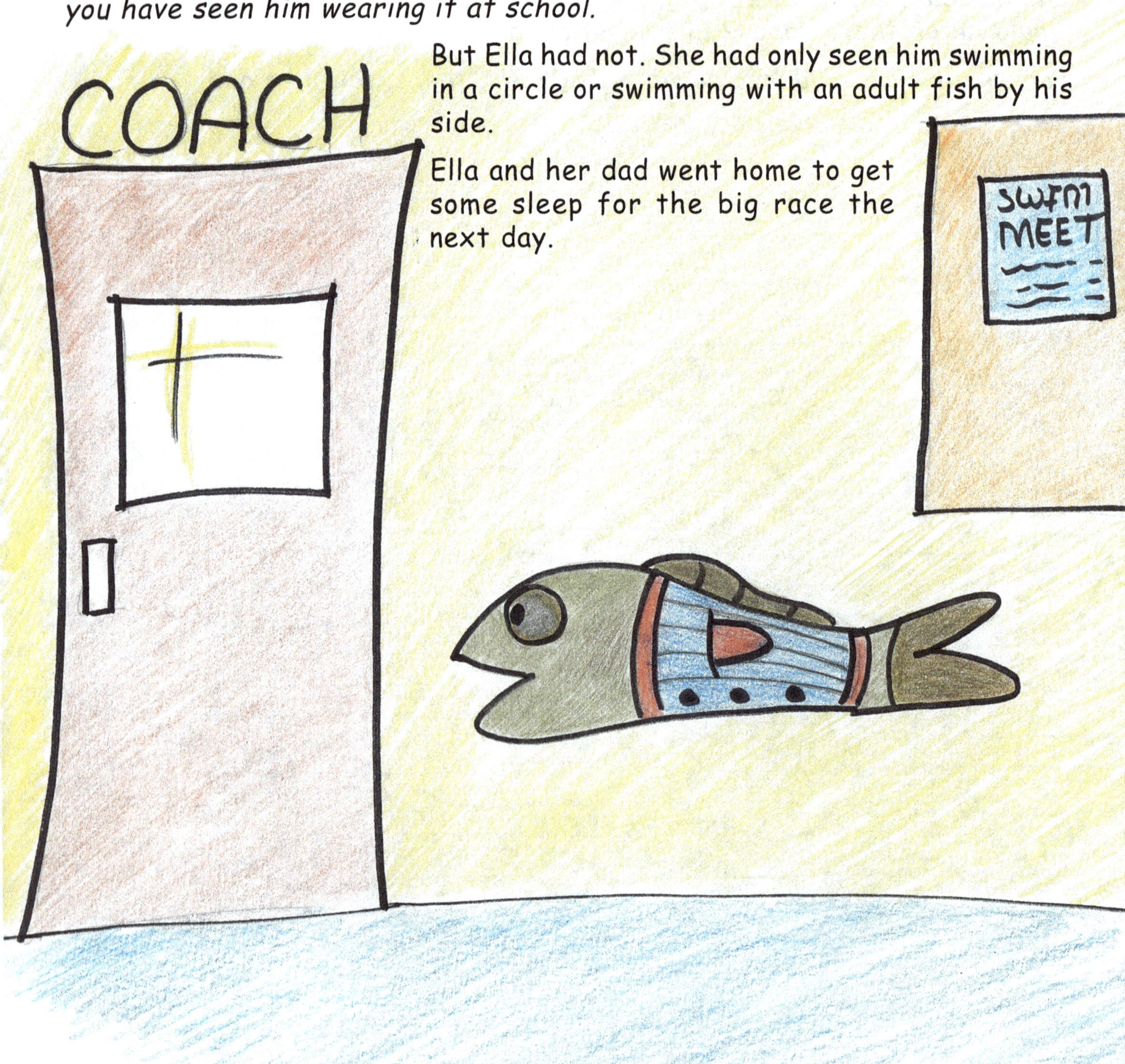

20

Rrrrring! Cried Ella's alarm clock. The big day was here and Ella jumped right up out of bed and swam downstairs for breakfast.

Good morning, Ella, said her mom with a great big smile. *Your breakfast is ready. You better eat so you have plenty of energy for the race today.*

Ella finished her breakfast and packed up her swimming gear and swam across the lake to the school for the swim meet.

21

Ella was so excited, she could hardly wait to get into the pool and race. There were many different fish from all over the lake. Ella swam up to the list to see what lane she would be in. She noticed that in the lane right next to her was her new friend Dylan.

I can't believe it! Dylan IS in the race. How can he race when he can't even swim straight? Ella asked herself as she looked at the list.

Suddenly, there was an announcement over the loud speaker.

"All elementary aged fish need to report to the pool area for the reading of the rules and gear check!"

It was time to get under way. As Ella stood there listening she was going over everything that Coach Stephens had taught her in her head.

Hey, Ella! Looks like we get to swim together, good luck! Ella turned around and there was Dylan.

Hey, Dylan, what is that you are wearing? Ella asked.

It's a special swim suit that my parents and doctors had made for me, it allows me to be a better swimmer. Dylan said.

The two lined up at the edge of the pool with the other swimmers ready to start the race. Ella had no idea how Dylan would swim, she just hoped that her friend would not be made fun of.

The next thing they heard was: *ready, set,* and then a loud whistle.

22

All of the swimmers dove into the pool and started swimming as fast as they could. Ella had one thing in mind and that was to win. She was not worried about anyone else and what they were doing. Something the coach had told her to do.

The fish swam back and forth across the pool for four laps and Ella felt pretty good about where she was. She made it to the end of the lane and she was so far ahead of everyone else that she had time to turn and cheer on her friends.

Go Emily! Go Belle! Go Kameron!

The she looked at the lane next to her and saw Dylan in third place.

Wow! Go Dylan! Faster, faster, faster! Ella shouted.

Dylan swam as fast as he could. Ella could not believe her eyes as Dylan came to the end of the pool and had kept his position in third place.

Dylan, that was awesome! How were you able to do that? I had no idea you could swim like that! She shouted as Dylan was catching his breath.

Sure I can. How else would I be on the swim team? He said as Ella's face turned red.

It's because I have this special swim suit. It helps me keep my balance when I swim and able to keep up with all of the other fish, said Dylan. I told you the other day that I could do basically everything you do except in a different way.

I am sorry Dylan, I didn't know that you meant everything. I am so proud of you for how well you did today, Ella told him.

There they stood side by side on the platform Ella in first place a boy from Laurel Lake Fish School in second and Dylan in third all three were smiling and standing so proud.

Ella learned a new lesson that day. Others may have disabilities or struggles but many times they are able to do the same things she can do, just in a different way.

From that day forward Ella and Dylan kept on racing and finishing in the top three at every event they went to. They not only became the best of friends and racing partners, but they volunteered to help other fish at the school that needed assistance.

The Truth About Disabilities

Many children are born with disabilities that keep them from doing things the same way as other children. Some children are born with very severe disabilities but many times they can make a difference in a person's life.

Many famous people were born with a disability or became disabled after an accident or illness. They did not let the disability stop them from achieving great things.

In 1776, Stephen Hopkins referred to his Cerebral Palsy when he signed the U.S. Declaration of Independence saying, "My hand trembles, but my heart does not."

Thomas Edison (1847-1931) was born with an overly large head and had developmental disabilities which slowed his early motor and language skills. Doctors claimed he would be "an invalid". Edison's school diagnosed him as "mentally ill" and "unteachable" because he could not complete his academic work. His mother Nancy Edison, a former teacher, removed her son from school and home-schooled him. She struggled to find methods to accommodate for Edison's developmental disabilities and dyslexia, and eventually found that Edison had to see and test things for himself. Edison went on to become one of the most recognized inventors of all the time.

Travis Free man went blind after a severe sinus infection. But he went on to play high school football, go to college at the University of Kentucky, and write a book about his life.

Remember when you see someone with a disability, don't stare or make them feel out of place, but make friends with them, like Ella did. They may just change your life.